Balboa Press books may be ordered through booksellers or by contacting:

Balboa Press
A Division of Hay House
1663 Liberty Drive
Bloomington, IN 47403
www.balboapress.com
1 (877) 407-4847

ISBN: 978-1-4525-2254-8 (sc)
ISBN: 978-1-4525-2255-5 (e)

Library of Congress Control Number: 2014916979

Print information available on the last page.

Balboa Press rev. date: 3/23/2015

BALBOA.
PRESS
A DIVISION OF HAY HOUSE

# Contents

1

# Molly McDougal Montgomery McGrath

Molly McDougal Montgomery McGrath
Doesn't like taking her daily bath.

She doesn't like washing her ankles and toes.
She doesn't like washing her ears or her nose.

She doesn't like soap. She doesn't like water.
She is the McGrath's dirtiest daughter.

Night after night she will loudly complain,
"I don't like the bathtub! I don't like the drain!"

"Oh, please!" said her mother. "Stop this commotion.
Such complaining strains a mother's devotion."

"I'm sorry," said Molly, "for causing you trouble.
I don't like the wash cloth. I don't like the bubbles."

"Enough!" said her sisters. "Too much!" said her father.
"How has taking a bath become such a bother?"

That's when the Clean Child Society was called
To settle this ruckus once and for all.

4

The Society came three o'clock that day,
With Mrs. McMurfus leading the way.

"Where is she?" she said. "This child unscrubbable,
This bath time Beelzebub who is otherwise loveable."

Then she saw Molly and said right away,
"This is a project that could last the day.

"This situation calls for serious action.
I'm going to need my clean child contraption."

She snapped her fingers and helpers arrived
With Child Scrubber Deluxe Model Nine-Eighty-Five.

"A grand machine," she said, heart filling with pride.
She opened the door and stepped right inside.

"Come here, dear child," she called. "You misguided creature,
We'll get things started with our hair washing feature.

"Would you like curls? Would you like a nice bob?
It can all be arranged by turning a knob."

A bowl appeared on a mechanical arm.
"Dear me!" said Molly. "Will it cause any harm?"

Mrs. McMurfus smiled as the bowl spun around
And landed on Molly with hardly a sound.

"You will shine," she said, "like a shimmering jewel.
It's easy to do. I have just the right tool.

"This glittering gizmo is really handy.
It will make you smell like peppermint candy."

Then soap started oozing from inside the bowl.
Lights started blinking on the master control.

"Smile," said a helper. "Our aim is to please.
Why, there's even a brush for cleaning your knees!

"And here is a feature that is really quite nice:
A left thumb-only cleaning device."

"That's silly!" cried Molly. "And what makes you suppose
That it's proper to bathe while wearing your clothes?"

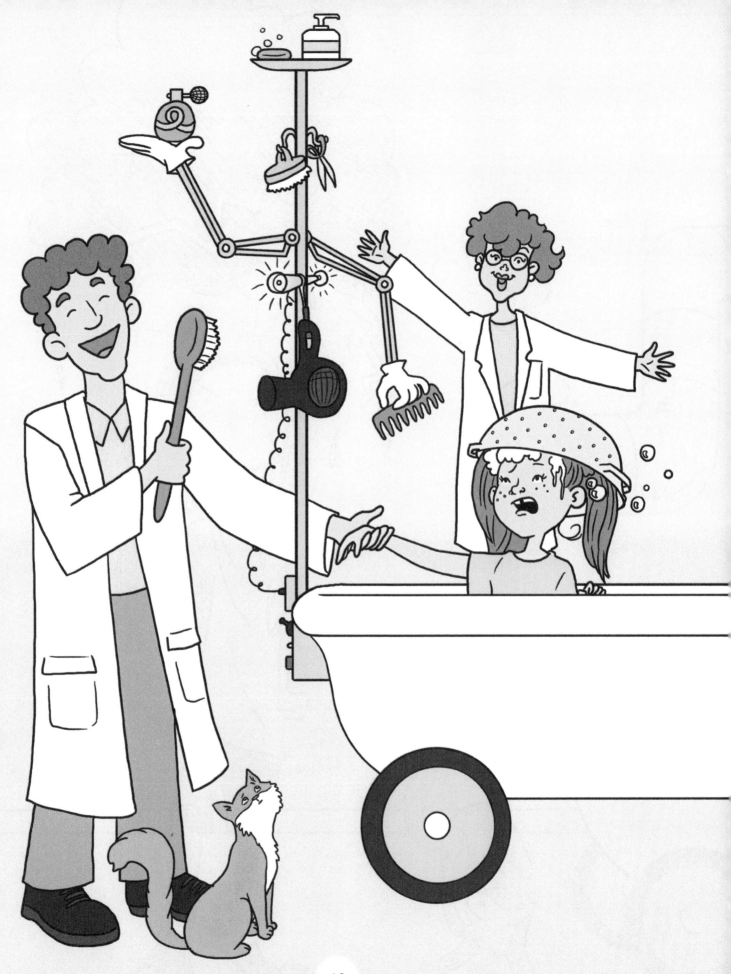

"Goodness!" said Mrs. McMurfus. "Everyone knows,
You can't clean a child without cleaning her clothes."

"We'll remove every smudge. We'll straighten each wrinkle.
It will all begin with a gentle spring sprinkle."

A dark cloud appeared and thunder roared.
It rained down on Molly and onto the floor.

"My rug!" cried Molly's mother. "My poor daughter!
Do you have a device for cleaning up water?"

"Oh, yes!" called the helpers. "That's part of our plan.
We will do it with help from our Number One Fan."

Fan Number One they turned up to level four.
It dried up the rug. It dried up the floor.

It dried up Molly. It fluffed up her cat.
It knocked her mother off the chair where she sat.

Mrs. McMurfus was overcome.
"Oh, joy!" she said. "Now isn't this fun?

"We'll have a grand time before we're done."
Then smoke started flowing from Fan Number One.

The entire contraption started to unglue.
It hiccupped and burped and began spitting goo.

The goo settled down like inky black snow.
It covered up Molly from her head to her toes.

The soot was so thick the decision was made
To call the captain of the Fire Brigade.

Mrs. McMurfus said, "There's no charge for today.
Ta-ta for now; I must be on my way."

She packed up Child Scrubber Nine-Eighty-Five,
Gathered her helpers and ran down the drive.

The captain arrived just seconds behind,
Not knowing what sort of disaster he'd find.

He ran in the house and there he found Molly.
"Oh, horror!" he gasped. "What unspeakable folly!"

21

"I'm afraid," he exclaimed, "there's nothing I can do.
This girl is covered in Child Scrubber Goo."

"This is a disaster," Molly's mother replied.
"Perhaps," said her father, "we should keep her outside."

The Captain explained, "This goo is unique.
It could last seven days or even a week.

"However," he warned, "I must make this clear.
Get her near soap, and it could last a year."

"No baths?" gasped her mother. "What will the neighbors say?"
"No baths?" said her father. "She'll scare them away."

"Ta-ta!" said the captain. "I really can't stay."
As Molly McGrath went outside to play.

She found a mucky spot covered with dust.
"This is perfect," she said. "A place I can trust."

For one glorious week she had the last laugh,
Miss Molly McDougal Montgomery McGrath.

# Bermuda Shorts

Last Saturday morning, as I lay in my bed,
I heard my Aunt Bertha and bald Uncle Fred.

"Wake up!" called my parents. "This is such a rare treat.
You're the luckiest boy on Sycamore Street."

"Come here!" said Aunt Bertha. "Come give me a squeeze."
Then she hugged me so hard that it buckled my knees.

She planted a sloppy wet kiss on my head,
Then handed me over to bald Uncle Fred.

"You've grown so," he said, as he started to laugh.
"You're no longer a boy. You're a boy and a half!"

Aunt Bertha whispered in Uncle Fred's ear.
She giggled so hard I'm surprised he could hear.

"Why, yes," he replied, with a gleam in his eyes.
"Right now would be splendid for such a surprise."

The next thing I saw, pointed right at my nose,
Was a bright blue box with big yellow bows.

The card on the gift said, "To a nephew true blue.
We want you to know we've been thinking of you."

I thanked them both, for I knew that I should.
Then I opened the box as fast as I could.

Lying before me, oh, how could this be true?
Was a polka dot nightmare in yellow and blue.

No doubt about it. I knew at a glance
I'd just received the world's ugliest pants.

32

Aunt Bertha was beaming and bursting with pride.
I felt really awful. I wanted to hide.

"Bermuda shorts," she said, "if you must know the truth,
Are an absolute must for the modern-day youth."

"That's right," said Uncle Fred, with a smile and a wink.
"Let's not overlook what the ladies will think."

"Young man," said my father, "I'm very impressed.
Not many your age are so stylishly dressed."

"My, my!" said Aunt Bertha. "It's such a nice day.
You can wear your new shorts when you go out to play."

"I won't do it!" I said. "There isn't a chance!
You can't make me wear those ridiculous pants!"

Uncle Fred looked astonished. Aunt Bertha looked sad.
My mom looked embarrassed. My father looked mad.

Their moment of joy had turned quickly to gloom.
"Young man!" said my father. "Please go to your room!"

"It's not fair," I said, as a tear filled my eye.
"Those shorts are just awful. I can't tell a lie."

I ran up the stairs and kicked open the door.
Then, just for good measure, I stomped on the floor.

"Bermudas," I cried, "are preposterous pants,
A curse put on children by uncles and aunts."

Just then, my father walked into the room.
I stared at the floor. I knew I was doomed.

"Aunt Bertha," he said, "is dazed and confused.
Her heart is broken. Her feelings are bruised.

"And poor Uncle Fred is filled with despair.
I'm telling you, Son, it just isn't fair.

"I'm not going to shout. I won't rant and rave.
But a young man your age should know how to behave."

Deep down in my heart, I had to admit,
I hadn't been nice, not one little bit.

We walked back downstairs, my father and I.
Though I put on a smile, I wanted to cry.

Aunt Bertha looked pale. Uncle Fred held her hand.
My mother was cooling her off with a fan.

"Those pants," I declared, "are one of a kind,
A wonderful treat, a marvelous find.

"I love my new shorts. I honestly do.
My favorite colors are yellow and blue.

"It was really unfair not to give them a chance.
Nothing lights up a room like polka dot pants."

"Oh, joy!" said Aunt Bertha. "I'm really relieved.
Those pants are quite special. I knew you'd be pleased."

Uncle Fred said, "By Godfrey! That makes me feel grand.
But those shorts aren't the only surprise we had planned."

"It's true," said Aunt Bertha. "Uncle Fred is quite right.
Today is a day of double delight.

"Turn around, my dear, and look over there.
Surprise number two is on top of that chair."

"Thank you," I said, as I lifted the lid.
"I know I must be the world's luckiest kid."

I stared in amazement at gift number two.
It seemed to be something in yellow and blue.

Oh, was there no end to the pain and the hurt?
Surprise number two was a polka dot shirt!

"Try it on," said my mom. "Please do," said my pop.
So I put on the shorts, I put on the top.

"Marvelous!" said Uncle Fred. "What a remarkable suit."
"What a doll," said Aunt Bertha. "Now, isn't he cute?"

My mother was certain I'd be a sensation,
So she sent me outside in that spotted creation.

"Show your friends," she said. "I know they'll be pleased."
"How could I," I thought, "without getting teased?"

I walked like a king. I tried to look proud.
Before very long, I attracted a crowd.

But lo and behold, that incredible day,
Not a soul in that crowd had a bad thing to say.

"Look!" they all cried. "That suit is fantastic."
They admired the fit and the sturdy elastic.

"Polka dots are the latest," I heard someone say.
"No doubt," said another. "They're the talk of the day!"

"That's right," I said. "If you must know the truth,
They're an absolute must for the modern-day youth."

Everyone agreed I looked pretty smart.
"That outfit," they said, "is a real work of art."

I must confess, I feel that way too.
My favorite colors are yellow and blue.

48

# The Beast, the Frog, my Friend, and I

When a big, blue frog swallowed my brother,
I did not tell my father or mother.
I thought that they might like to know,
But I knew that they would worry so.

I did not scream. I did not shout.
I asked the frog to spit him out.
The frog agreed. I knew he would.
My brother doesn't taste so good.

When zombies gathered at Fourth and Main,
I did not holler or complain.
"Please leave," I said. "Don't make a fuss.
I'll arrange for you to take a bus."

They all went home as evening fell.
I bid the group a fond farewell.
Where they went, I'll never tell.
I keep a secret very well.

But sometimes secrets get away.
It happened just the other day.
My best friend whispered in my ear
A secret she thought I should hear.

She told me, when she gets the chance,
She likes to do a silly dance.
She wears her mother's floppy hat
And dances with the family cat.

Somehow, her secret just got out.
From ear to ear, it danced about.
It wasn't me. I didn't tell.
I keep a secret very well.

When a kissing fish kissed Shirley Schwartz,
I found nothing special to report.
The situation was alarming,
But Shirley found the fish quite charming.

He would entertain her daily.
He'd sing and play the ukulele.
Shirley read him travel books
About lagoons with cozy nooks.

Then one day they slipped away
To spend their life at Mango Bay.
My lips are sealed. I will not tell.
I keep a secret very well.

Sometimes secrets are such fun.
Today, I heard another one.
My best friend said, "Come very close.
I'll tell you who I like the most."

She said that she liked Freddy Flynn,
That redhead with the devilish grin.
He is not cute. He is not smart.
Yet somehow, Freddy won her heart.

But someone set her secret free.
Heaven knows, it was not me.
That's not something that I would tell.
I keep a secret pretty well.

When a spaceship landed Friday night,
I found the crew was most polite.
They asked, "Who might your leader be?"
Of course, I told them it was me.

I politely introduced myself.
I wished them happiness and good health.
I offered them a late-night snack
And said, "I hope you do come back."

They left and took some people with them.
I hope their families do not miss them.
I promised that I would not tell.
I keep a secret pretty well.

My best friend frowns and sometimes pouts
When people let her secrets out.
Her name is Florence Flugelhorn Fontaine,
Although she really hates her middle name.

I promised I would never tell,
But things did not turn out so well.
For some reason every kid in town
Would giggle when she came around.

"Miss Flugelhorn," I heard them say.
Then they would laugh and run away.
I don't know how this ever started.
People can be so cold-hearted.

My friend said, "Secrets that get out
Are secrets I've told you about."
"Oh, no," I said. "I'd never tell.
I keep a secret fairly well."

I told her a fire-breathing beast
Comes to all our family feasts.
"Oh, stop!" she said. "Please do be quiet.
Not one more tale, I will not buy it.

"There's no blue frog or rocket ship.
I don't trust what passes from your lips.
There is no fire-breathing beast,
I don't believe you in the least."

Maybe, possibly, it could be true
That I've let slip a secret or two.
But tell a tale, an outright lie,
I tell you, I would rather die.

"I'm sorry," I told my best friend.
"I hope our friendship never ends.
But secrets are so very clever.
I cannot keep them trapped forever."

Just then, a fire-breathing beast
Stopped to chat as he headed east.
He was well-mannered and well-dressed.
He wore a top hat and a vest.

He said, "It is time for cookies and tea.
I do hope you'll be joining me."
He had sugar cookies in his vest.
He heated a teapot with his breath.

My best friend joined in and raised her cup.
And that's when she was swallowed up.
A big, blue frog was passing by
And mistook her for a butterfly.

I told him, "Butterflies have wings.
You should be mindful of such things."
He agreed that's something he should know.
And so, in time, he let her go.

My friend said, "What a rude thing to do."
She was covered up in froggy goo.
She said, "I do apologize
For saying that your tales were lies."

"Oh, no," I said, "I've no excuse.
I heard your secrets and set them loose.
Secrets seem to flow through me
Like wind that passes through a tree."

And then we hugged and had a cry,
The beast, the frog, my friend, and I.
They told me that they thought it best
To let a sleeping secret rest.

"I'll try," I said. "I hope I do.
I'm lucky to have friends like you.
The honest truth is sad to tell:
I don't keep a secret very well."

# Fedora Flats

More than anything else in Fedora Flats,
Folks love showing off their marvelous hats.

Colorful hats in all shapes and sizes.
Hats that have won a ton of first prizes.

Fabulous hats with bright orange feathers.
Hats you can wear in all kinds of weather.

Children's hats that look like cotton candy.
Hats filled with tools for the man who is handy.

Bertha Bunchbean's turban is twenty times her height.
A searchlight on the top helps her see at night.

Fred Flubman's porcupine looks a bit like Fred.
He combs it with great care and wears it on his head.

Each day at the square in the center of town,
Hats are put on and paraded around.

Turbans and derbies, top hats and bonnets,
Each made unique by the things that are on it.

One of a kind and kind of a wonder.
Hats you would beam with pride to stand under.

Some are fashioned with fruit. Some are covered with chimes.
A few come with clocks that keep perfect time.

Trinkets and tinsel, doodads and spangles,
Baubles placed at the oddest of angles.

The hats of the Flats make a stunning display.
But someone did something to take them away.

Percival Pompadour, like the rest of his clan,
Does not picture himself a hat-wearing man.

He knows others like hats, but he just doesn't care.
He does not like devices that crumple his hair.

His hair is a marvel, each follicle a prize,
Their wavy perfection a treat for the eyes.

He combs his fine hair, each fabulous layer,
In a hair style he feels is fit for a mayor.

The good folks of the Flats cannot recall
Having voted for Percival at all.

But one small group with one tiny complaint
Thought Percival Pompadour was a saint.

The Ladies League for Fine Fruit and Flowers
Wanted to ban prunes, but did not have the power.

They wanted a mayor who did not like prunes.
"And we got what we wanted," said Velvet von Doon.

"He dislikes prune Danish, does not like stewed prunes.
He does not like the sight of a prune on his spoon."

Percival banished all prunes from the Flats,
But the ladies were shocked when he also banned hats.

"No beanies," he said, "or ten gallon hats.
No straw hats or bowlers. I want nothing like that.

"No delicate hats with gossamer wings.
No busy berets. I want none of those things.

84

"And as for that teapot Velvet wears on her head,
From now on it will rest on a table instead."

Ban her pink teapot with lavender rings?
How could Percival do such a terrible thing?

Ban hats? Why not ban the sun from the sky?
The townsfolk were numb. They wanted to cry.

"To me," said Fred Flubman, "the answer is clear.
My porcupine whispered this thought in my ear:

"We will build him a hat with love and great care.
A glorious hat that won't mess up his hair.

"Something that will test our hat-making skills.
He will learn to love hats. I just know that he will."

"To hold up such a hat," said Velvet von Doon,
"We will certainly need an enormous balloon."

"We'll need cloth," cried the town. "Red, purple, green and blue.
We'll need lots of glitter and a large vat of glue."

They built a little bit, and then a little more,
And before they knew it, they'd built a second floor.

They glued peacock feathers and roses by the score.
They did way too much, then did a whole lot more.

They put a statue of Percival on the top.
The hat was so fantastic they just couldn't stop.

A fountain and some plants were added to the list,
Along with some knick-knacks they surely would not miss.

Blinking lights were added and baubles from the past.
Colored yarn was strung, but the best they saved for last.

A banner went on top. Quotations were discussed.
The words that they chose were, "In Percival We Trust."

When Percival saw the hat, he gasped with delight.
The colors were perfect. The style was just right.

A balloon held the hat. The hat framed his face,
A marvelous design that kept his hair in place.

A strap was tightly fastened underneath his chin,
And just then he noticed a little gust of wind.

Percival's hat was lifted straight up in the air.
Then he floated away with his marvelous hair.

Some said, "What a pity. It's a shame that he's gone."
Most folks simply smiled as their hats went back on.

He floated down several counties away,
And it's there he remains to this very day.

He lives a life filled with happiness there,
Married to a woman who admires his hair.

Everyone is happy, even Velvet von Doon,
Who was recently spotted eating a prune.

CPSIA information can be obtained at www.ICGtesting.com
Printed in the USA
BVOW10s2132080415

395386BV00003B/4/P